Hi Ben!

You're Super Strong!

Brian Broccoli

Name:	Brian Broccoli
Super Power:	Super Strong
Height:	26" (stem to stalk)
Color:	Dark green
Location:	The Great Glass Greenhouse
Hobbies:	Working out, weight-lifting, playing electric guitar, rock-collecting
Favorite Snack:	Broccoli with hummus

MISSION

Brian Broccoli will need all of his Super Strength to stop a Greasy Grease cart from destroying the fresh food at the Farmer's Market!

SPROWTZ FILES

This book is dedicated to a future filled with strong and healthy children.

THIS BOOK WAS PRINTED IN THE USA

Super Sprowtz™, ™, A Nutrition Education Series™,
Brian Broccoli and all related titles, logos, and characters are trademarks of Super Sprowtz LLC.

Copyright © 2010 by Super Sprowtz LLC.

Created by Radha Agrawal

Written by Radha Agrawal and Jessie Jenkins

Illustrations © 2010 by Super Sprowtz LLC.

Illustrations by Archie Valdez

Cover art by Kenny Velez and Archie Valdez

Vegetable photography by Bill Levey

All Rights Reserved.

Published in the United States of America by
Super Sprowtz LLC, P.O. Box 500, New York, NY 10014

www.supersprowtz.com

ISBN-13 978-0-9844845-2-2 ISBN-10 0-9844845-2-3

WOR 10 9 8 7 6 5 4 3 2 1

The Super Sprowtz

I AM BRIAN BROCCOLI AND I AM SUPER STRONG!

created by Radha Agrawal

written by Radha Agrawal and Jessie Jenkins

illustrated by Archie Valdez

Isle OF
Pollution

Super S...
H...
...

Brian B...
daily wor...
S...

Rayne's
soccer

It was a hot and muggy summer day in the City.
Brian Broccoli scratched the great big mound
of green on his head.

Scratch, scratch, scratch.

He had forgotten to jump under Rayne's watering
can after his morning workout, so he was feeling quite itchy.

Out of the corner of his eye, he noticed Rayne struggling to carry a giant
bag of soil into the Great Glass Greenhouse.

"Rayne," he boomed. "Did you forget that I am Super Strong? Let me help you!"
He ran over and easily picked up the giant bag, hoisting it overhead with
one muscular arm. "Where do you need this to go?"

The greenhouse rattled as he spoke. Even his *voice* was Super Strong!

Rayne smiled sheepishly. It had been several weeks since lightning
struck the Great Glass Greenhouse and brought her vegetable garden
to life. She was still getting used to her new super-powered friends.

"Right in the corner would be great," she replied.

Brian Broccoli walked the bag to the back of the greenhouse,
past Oliver Onion and Gita Garlic who were holding hands
and gazing adoringly at each other.

"Thanks, Brian Broccoli!" said Rayne.

She leaned over close to Brian Broccoli's big green head and whispered, "What are their Super Powers again?"

Brian Broccoli smiled. "They're Super Sweet," he said.

Rayne looked confused.

"Their hearts are super powerful! They can neutralize anything that is bad for the heart. You planted them next to each other and, well, they've been inseparable ever since! In fact, their super powers only work when they're holding hands."

All of a sudden, a deafening sound filled the Great Glass Greenhouse.

Whoop, whoop! Whoop, whoop!

"What's that noise?" Rayne shouted, covering her ears.

"That's our Super Alarm! Colby Carrot must have
spotted trouble!" Brian Broccoli yelled back as
he ran towards the toolshed that led to the
Super Sprowtz Headquarters.

Colby Carrot had been perched on the roof of
the Great Glass Greenhouse all morning, scanning
the city for trouble with his Super Sight.

After sounding the Super Alarm,
he slid down his Super Slide
into Headquarters.

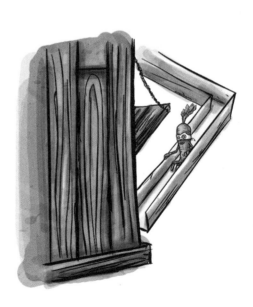

Rayne watched as the rest of the Super Sprowtz dropped what they were doing and dashed towards the toolshed.

She was still amazed that their high-tech Headquarters were somehow hidden inside Grandpa Wyse's plain old shed!

After the last of the Super Sprowtz disappeared into the shed, Rayne poked her head through the rabbit hole that served as the entrance to Headquarters.

The Super Sprowtz were gathered around the hovering image of a greasy giant in the hologram at the center of the room.

"Greasy is up to no good again!" said Colby Carrot gravely. "I spotted him pushing a Greasy Grease Cart towards the Farmer's Market! It looks like it's another one of his booby-trapped carts! If Greasy Grease explodes onto the market, it will destroy all the delicious food!"

Greasy worked for Pompous Pollution, the Super Sprowtz's archenemy.
Greasy Grease was made in one of Pompous Pollution's many factories.
Pompous believed that all food should be covered in Greasy Grease - even the
fresh vegetables at the Farmer's Market!

Erica Eggplant's super brain had quickly come up with a plan. "Brian Broccoli!"
she ordered. "You're the only one strong enough to stop that cart. Suzy Sweetpea
can get you there, but you'll need to use your Super Strength to keep that
grease-filled cart from reaching the Farmer's Market! Take Oliver Onion
and Gita Garlic with you. Their Super Hearts can neutralize the Greasy Grease!"

Brian Broccoli leapt up, ready to go.

Erica Eggplant handed him an earpiece and said, "Don't forget to stay in contact with Headquarters! We will be following your every move."

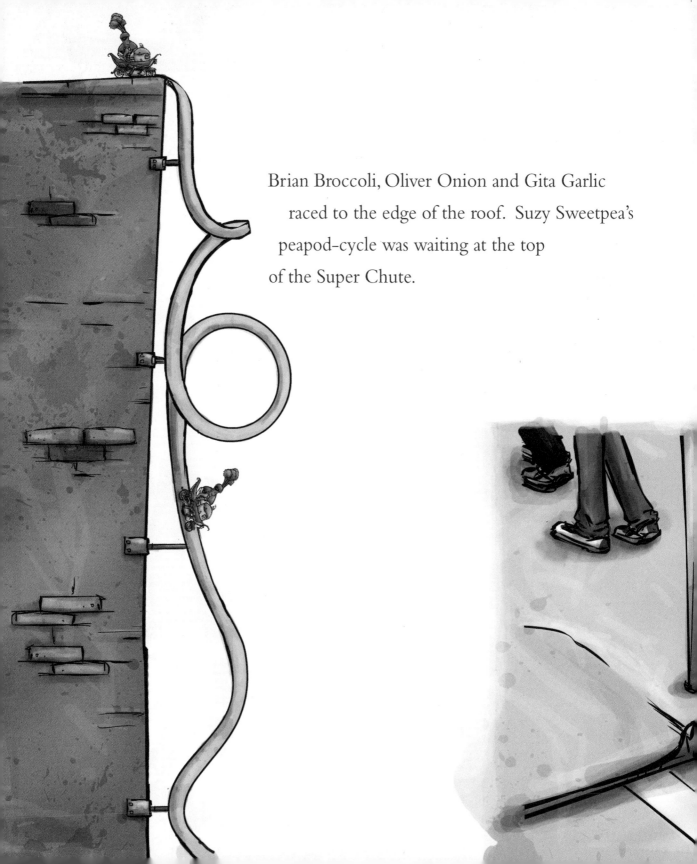

Brian Broccoli, Oliver Onion and Gita Garlic
raced to the edge of the roof. Suzy Sweetpea's
peapod-cycle was waiting at the top
of the Super Chute.

Safety first! Suzy Sweetpea made sure that everyone strapped on the coconut helmets that Rayne had thoughtfully made for them.

They all piled in and the peapod-cyle took off, with Suzy Sweetpea expertly navigating the hairpin turns in the Super Chute as it dropped 47 stories to the street below. The peapod-cycle hit the street and headed downtown.

Within minutes, they had Greasy and his gruesomely greasy cart in their sights. They watched in horror as he gave the cart one final shove towards the bustling market and disappeared into the crowd.

From back at Headquarters, Erica Eggplant buzzed in Brian Broccoli's ear.

"Forget about Greasy, just stop that cart!"

Suzy Sweetpea zoomed even faster and pulled the peapod-cycle alongside the cart.

The Super Sweethearts held hands tightly as Brian Broccoli picked them up and, with one Super Strong toss, catapulted them towards the fast moving cart. Never letting go of each other, they disappeared inside.

"Suzy Sweetpea!" shouted Brian Broccoli. "Get me about a block past that cart, pronto!" Suzy Sweetpea sped up and, moments later, Brian Broccoli jumped out of the peapod-cycle. "I'll pick you up on the other side of the market!" she yelled as she zoomed off.

Turning to face the hurtling cart, Brian Broccoli stretched out his Super Strong arms and braced himself for impact when suddenly...

BAM!

WHOOOOOSH!

The Greasy Grease cart hit a pothole in the middle of the street! It flew into the air and sailed right over Brian Broccoli's head!

"Sprowtz Headquarters, do you copy?" Brian Broccoli yelled into his earpiece. "I've got a problem!"

"We know," Erica Eggplant crackled back. "And I've got more bad news! Colby Carrot saw the whole thing with his Super Sight. Oliver Onion and Gita Garlic were separated by the impact and can't use their Super Sweet hearts!"

Brian Broccoli, who was now chasing after the cart as fast as his Super Strong legs would carry him, shouted back, "what now?"

He began to worry. The cart would reach the crowded market in seconds!

The earpiece crackled again.

"Brian Broccoli, we're going to have to cover that cart before it explodes! Can you see the red tent over the bakery stand? By my calculations, the cart will pass under that tent in 3.8 seconds. Can you get there in time?"

Brian Broccoli knew he wasn't going
to make it.

Suddenly, he had an idea.
Reaching up, he broke off two big
broccoli stalks from his head. Within seconds,
two new stalks grew in their place.

He aimed the stalks at the poles holding up the
tent and threw them with all his might.

The broccoli stalks hit the poles with a bang and the tent collapsed, completely covering the greasy time bomb!

Only Brian Broccoli could throw a piece of broccoli hard enough to bring down a bakery tent!

Brian Broccoli skidded to a halt next to
the cart and held his breath
as it began to shake.

There was no sign of Gita Garlic and Oliver Onion.
Would they reunite in time to neutralize
the Greasy Grease?

KABOOM!

The tent flew off the top of the cart and a beautiful fountain of water shot up into the sky. Oliver Onion and Gita Garlic had found each other and neutralized the grease! Holding hands, they sailed gracefully through the air and landed safely in Brian Broccoli's outstretched arms.

Everyone at Super Sprowtz Headquarters cheered. The farmers clapped their hands as the hot and dusty fruits and vegetables were rinsed clean by the spraying water. Children ran in and out of the falling water laughing and playing.

Suzy Sweetpea pulled into the market to gather up the Sprowtz and head for home, but she couldn't find Brian Broccoli anywhere!

AHA! There he was - standing under the last of the cool, clean water, finally getting his long-awaited shower.

Meet Brian Broccoli - he is Super Strong!

Eating broccoli helps make your child super strong because it's filled with bone-strengthening calcium, the powerful antioxidant sulforaphane and immune system-boosting vitamin C.

Calcia-who? Sulfora-what? Immuna-where?

Clams and mussels use calcium to build strong shells, but for humans it's the essential material for building bones. And sulforaphane? That's an organic compound that is believed to fight cancer and battle bacterial infection. And good old vitamin C helps your immune system stay strong to help heal cuts and bruises faster and keep you and your child from getting sick. Eating broccoli has also been linked to prevention of heart disease.

Did you know that broccoli was first cultivated in Europe around 2,000 years ago? Since the days of the Roman Empire, it has been particularly popular in Italy - in fact, the word broccoli comes from "broccolo" meaning "the flowering top of a cabbage."

How do you know which Super Strong broccoli to choose at the store? Look for broccoli that is dark green, sage or even purple and has a firm stalk. Stay away from yellowing broccoli or heads with flowers since this is a sign that it is past its prime. Try steaming broccoli for six minutes instead of boiling. Steaming will keep this super food green and crisp and full of all of its cancer-fighting power!

For an easy and delicious way to prepare broccoli, try Chef Youkilis' Super Strong broccoli recipe on the next page!

Super Strong Broccoli, Carrot and Mozzarella Salad
Chef Scott Youkilis

Serves: 4   Time: 30 minutes   Level: Easy

2 heads broccoli, florets removed and cut into bite-sized pieces
1 bunch of carrots, cut into bite-sized pieces
1/4 cup extra virgin olive oil
1/2 cup pecans, roughly chopped
1 lemon, juiced
1 kid's handful of Italian parsley leaves, coarsely chopped
1 avocado
3/4 cup shredded organic mozzarella
Salt and pepper

Preheat oven to 400°F.

Toss half of the olive oil with the carrots and broccoli and place on a cookie sheet. Season with salt and pepper. Cook for 12-14 minutes or until veggies start to soften slightly but are not cooked completely through. Add pecans and cook for another 5-7 minutes or until nuts are toasted. Remove from oven and place in bowl. Add remaining oil, lemon juice, parsley and cheese. Garnish with sliced avocado.

View how-to video and post your favorite cooking pictures at supersprowtz.com!

Chef Scott Youkilis is a new father, chef and owner of two award-winning restaurants in San Francisco – Maverick and Hog & Rocks. He is dedicated to supporting the development of local food systems and sources the highest quality veggies grown in his home state of California. By doing so, he hopes to ensure that all kids and adults will live happier and healthier lives.

BROCCOLI - SUPER STRONG

A Super Food! Full of nutrients, antioxidants and vitamins including A, K, and immune system-boosting vitamin C. Also contains calcium, which is important for strong bones and phytonutrients which may have anti-cancer effects.

CARROTS - SUPER SIGHT

Rich in beta-carotene, which the body converts to vitamin A. Vitamin A promotes good vision – especially at night!

EGGPLANT - SUPER SMART

Purple and blue vegetables and fruits like eggplant have phytochemicals that are good for memory. Eggplant also contains nasunin, which protects brain cell membranes. Eggplant is rich in antioxidants that can reduce the risk of cancer.

PEAS - SUPER SPEED

Contain lots of vitamins and minerals, as well as dietary fiber and protein. Green peas are a great source of energy!

ONION AND GARLIC - SUPER SWEET

Both contain sulfides, which may lower blood lipids and blood pressure and help protect against heart disease.

ZUCCHINI - SUPER SWIMMER

Full of water, zucchini also contains folate and other B vitamins, which have numerous health benefits, including lowering bad cholesterol and improving lipid profiles.

SPINACH - SUPER STRETCHY

Packed with nutrients, spinach is a rich source of vitamins A and K and many antioxidants, as well as minerals such as calcium, magnesium, manganese and iron.

TOMATO - SUPER SAFE

Technically a fruit, tomatoes contain significant amounts of vitamin C and lycopene, which have antioxidant and cancer-preventing properties.

MUSHROOMS - SUPER SOOTHING

These members of the fungi kingdom provide a significant amount of potassium, a mineral that helps the body maintain normal heart rhythm, fluid balance and muscle function.

Please note, never let your child eat mushrooms they find in the wild! Only experts can distinguish edible mushrooms from poisonous ones.

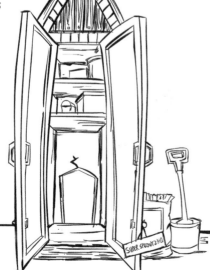

For more information, visit supersprowtz.com!

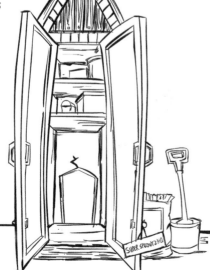

GLOSSARY

RADHA AGRAWAL

Radha is the creator of Super Sprowtz. She passionately believes that the current conversation with children about food isn't working. After opening Slice, an organic pizzeria, with her twin sister, Radha became a regular visitor to New York City public schools where she spoke about nutrition and healthy living. Alarmed by what she saw as a growing obesity epidemic among urban children, she became deeply committed to changing the way children eat. This, combined with her years of experience in story-telling as a commercial and film producer led her to create the Super Sprowtz. It is her belief that through entertaining story lines, catchy music, and lovable characters, children can see vegetables and nutrition differently. She earned her Bachelor of Science degree from Cornell University where she also played Varsity soccer. She currently lives, paints, bikes and eats locally (likely at Slice) in New York City.

JESSIE JENKINS

Jessie brings her love for healthy eating, her belief in sustainable food systems and her commitment to education to Super Sprowtz. Born and raised in New York City, Jessie taught ninth-grade science in Manhattan's Washington Heights, a neighborhood where 95% of the students qualify for the city's free-lunch program and 21% of adults are obese. While teaching, she created and fully funded the Learning Garden project - a rooftop classroom where teachers integrated gardening into their curricula. Jessie holds a BA in Environmental Studies from Oberlin College and a Masters in Science Education from Teachers College Columbia University. She lives and gardens in Brooklyn, New York.

ARCHIE P. VALDEZ

Archie P. Valdez has created art for video games, books, graphic novels, animations and commercials. Originally from the Philippines, Archie was raised in Nigeria before moving to the U.S. He studied art in San Francisco at the Academy of Art University, where he earned his Bachelor of Fine Arts with a focus in animation and illustration. Archie was initially a music and chemistry major and is still passionate about those fields - you can hear him singing sometimes when he works. Archie likes to travel, cook (in moderation), play video games and various sports, and drink coffee while sketching. He also loves to watch cartoons. Archie lives in New York City. He loves finding delicious snacks to munch on at the Farmer's Market in Union Square.

Now Available

The Super Sprowtz: Origins!

I Am Brian Broccoli and I Am Super Strong!

I Am Erica Eggplant and I Am Super Smart!

Coming Soon

I Am Colby Carrot and I Have Super Sight!

I Am Suzy Sweetpea and I Have Super Speed!

I Am Todd Tomato and I Am Super Safe!

I Am Miki Mushroom and I Am Super Soothing!

I Am Sammy Spinach and I Am Super Stretchy!

I Am Zach Zucchini and I Am a Super Swimmer!

We Are Oliver Onion and Gita Garlic and We Are Super Sweet!